The Golden Goose

By Jacob and Wilhelm Grimm
Illustrated by Dorothée Duntze
Adapted by Anthea Bell

North-South Books

Once upon a time there was a man who had three sons. The youngest was known as Simpleton and he was scorned and mocked and slighted at every opportunity. It happened that the eldest son wanted to go into the forest to cut wood. Before he went, his mother gave him a beautiful sweet cake and a bottle of wine to take with him, so that he wouldn't be hungry or thirsty.

When he came to the forest, he met a little, gray old man, who wished him good day and said, "Do give me a piece of your cake and let me drink a sip of your wine; I'm so hungry and thirsty."

However, the clever son said, "If I give you my cake and my wine I'll have nothing for myself, so be off with you."

And he left the little man standing there and went his way. But when he began to cut down a tree it wasn't long before he missed his stroke, and cut his arm with the ax, so that he had to go home and have it bound up. That was the little gray man's doing.

Then the second son went off to the forest, and his mother gave him a sweet cake and a bottle of wine, just like his brother. The little, gray old man met him as well, and asked for a piece of his cake and a sip of his wine.

The second son too said, sensibly enough, "Anything I give you I won't have for myself, so be off with you." And he left the little man standing there and went his way.

He was soon to get his punishment, for when he had swung his ax at a tree a couple of times he cut his own leg and had to be carried home.

So then Simpleton said, "Father, do let me go out to cut wood."

"Your brothers have hurt themselves cutting wood," said his ther, "so you'd better not try; you don't know anything about oodcutting."

However, Simpleton went on and on asking until at last his father said, "Oh, very well, off you go, and if you hurt yourself it'll teach you a lesson." His mother gave him a cake made with water and baked in the ashes, and a bottle of sour beer.

When Simpleton came to the forest he too met the little, gray old man, who wished him good day and then said, "Give me a piece of your cake and a drink from your bottle; I'm so hungry and thirsty."

"I've nothing but a cake baked in the ashes and some sour beer," said Simpleton, "but if you don't mind that, let's sit down and eat."

So they sat down, and when Simpleton brought out his cake baked in the ashes, it was a fine sweet cake, and the sour beer was good wine.

Well, they ate and they drank, and then the little man said, "Since you have a kind heart and are willing to share what you have, I will give you good fortune. There's an old tree over there. Cut it down and you'll find something among its roots." And with these words the little man went away.

Simpleton went and cut the tree down, and as it fell he saw a goose with feathers of pure gold sitting among the roots. He picked the goose up, took it away with him, and went into an inn to spend the night there. The innkeeper had three daughters, who were

curious about this wonderful bird and longed to have one of its golden feathers.

"I'm sure I'll find some chance to pluck a feather from the bird," thought the eldest.

And when Simpleton had gone out of the room she took hold of the goose's wing, but her hand and her fingers stuck to it.

Soon afterward the innkeeper's second daughter came in, also planning to get a golden feather. However, no sooner had she touched her sister than she stuck fast too.

Finally the third daughter came in with the same idea in mind, whereupon the others cried out, "Keep away, for heaven's sake, keep away!"

But she didn't see any reason to keep away. "If they're both plucking feathers, so will I," she thought. So up she came, and when she had touched her sister she stuck fast too. So they had to spend all night with the goose.

The next day Simpleton picked up his goose and went away, taking no notice of the three girls hanging on behind. They had to keep running along after him, going left or right, whichever way he went himself.

Out in the countryside the parson met them, and when he saw this procession he said, "You bold girls, you ought to be ashamed of yourselves, running after a young fellow like that! Is this any way to behave?"

With these words, he took the youngest girl by the hand to pull her away, but as soon as he touched her he stuck fast too, and had to run along behind them all himself.

Before long the sexton came by and saw the parson following the three girls. He called out, in surprise, "Hello, your reverence, and where are you off to in such a hurry? Don't forget there's a christening today!" And he went up to him and took him by the sleeve, but then he was stuck too.

As the five of them trotted along after one another, two farmers came out of the fields with their spades. The parson shouted out to them and told them to pull him and the sexton free. But no sooner had they touched the sexton than they were stuck as well, so now there were seven of them all running after Simpleton and his goose.

Then he came to a city ruled by a King whose daughter had so serious a nature that no one could ever make her laugh. So the King had proclaimed that anyone who could make her laugh should marry her.

When Simpleton heard that, he took his goose and her followers and went before the King's daughter, and when she saw the seven people running along behind one another, she began to laugh so heartily she couldn't stop.

Then Simpleton asked for her hand in marriage, but the King did not like the idea of having him for a son-in-law and made all kinds of objections, saying that first he must bring him a man who could drink a cellar full of wine.

Simpleton remembered the little gray man, and thought he could probably help him. He went out into the forest, and when he came to the place where he had cut the tree down he saw a man sitting there looking very sorry for himself.

Simpleton asked what the matter was, and the man said, "I have such a thirst, and I can't quench it, for I can't abide cold water. I drank up a barrel of wine, but what's a drop of water falling on a hot stone?"

"I can help you there," said Simpleton. "Just come with me and you shall have enough to quench your thirst."

Simpleton then led the thirsty man to the King's cellar, and the man set to work on the great barrels in it, drinking and drinking until his middle hurt him. Before the day was over he had drunk the whole cellar full of wine.

Then Simpleton asked for his bride again, but the King was angry to think of a foolish fellow known to everyone as Simpleton carrying off his daughter. He made more conditions: first, said he, Simpleton must bring him a man who could eat a whole mountain of bread.

Simpleton wasted no time, but went straight off to the forest, and there, in the very same place, he found a man tightening a leather belt around his waist and looking very sorry for himself.

"I've just eaten a whole oven full of bread rolls," said he, "but what's that to a man as hungry as I am? My stomach's still empty, and all I can do is belt my waist in to keep myself from dying of starvation."

Simpleton was glad to hear it, and said, "Come with me and you can eat until you're full." And he took him to the court of the King, who had had all the flour in his kingdom brought there and baked into a huge mountain of bread. The man he had met in the forest set to work to eat it, and within a day the whole mountain was gone.

So now Simpleton asked for his bride for the third time, but the King was still looking for some way out, and said that first he must have a ship that could go both on land and on water. "And as soon as you sail up in it," said he, "you shall have my daughter for your wife."

Simpleton went straight off to the forest, and there sat the little, gray old man to whom he had given his cake.

"I have drunk for you, and eaten for you," said the little gray man, "and now I'll give you the ship as well, because you took pity on me."

So he gave him a ship that could go both on land and on water, and when the King saw it, he could no longer refuse to let Simpleton marry his daughter.

Then the wedding was held, and after the King's death Simpleton inherited his kingdom. He and his wife lived happily together for many years.

First published in the United States, Great Britain, Canada,
Australia, and New Zealand in 1988 by North-South Books,
an imprint of Nord-Süd Verlag AG, Gossau Zürich, Switzerland.
First paperback edition published in 1999.

Distributed in the United States by North-South Books Inc., New York.

Library of Congress Cataloging-in-Publication Data
Goldene Gans. English
The golden goose.
Translation of: Die goldene Gans
Summary: Simpleton's generosity helps him gain a princess for his bride.
[1. Fairy tales. 2. Folklore—Germany]
I. Grimm, Jacob, 1785-1863. II. Grimm, Wilhelm, 1786-1859.
III. Bell, Anthea. IV. Duntze, Dorothée, ill. V. Title
PZ8.G55 1988 [398.2] 87-32108

British Library Cataloguing-in-Publication Data
Grimm, Jacob
The golden goose.
1. Tales—Germany
I. Title II. Grimm, Wilhelm III. Duntze, Dorothée
IV. Die goldene Gans. *English*
398.2'1'0943 PZ8.1

ISBN 0-7358-1198-9
1 3 5 7 9 10 8 6 4 2
Printed in Belgium

For more information about our books,
and the authors and artists who create them,
visit our web site: http://www.northsouth.com

Using Picture Books

to Teach Writing With the Traits

An Annotated Bibliography of More Than 200 Titles With Teacher-Tested Lessons

by Ruth Culham

NEW YORK • TORONTO • LONDON • AUCKLAND • SYDNEY
MEXICO CITY • NEW DELHI • HONG KONG • BUENOS AIRES

Teaching Resources

DEDICATION

...y friend and editor, Ray Coutu, and his beautiful son, Joseph

ACKNOWLEDGMENTS

Many thanks to the teachers who contributed their ideas for books and lessons for this text, especially Lynne Riddick, Columbia, South Carolina; Sean O'Day, Columbia, South Carolina; Colleen Vollmers, Detroit Lakes, Minnesota; Pam Daly, Detroit Lakes, Minnesota; Linda Kinane, Albuquerque, New Mexico; Lin Steele, Pahrump, Nevada; and Jim Blasingame, Tempe, Arizona. And a sincere thank you to all the teachers and administrators who have sent book selections and lesson ideas to me over the years. Keep them coming. I hope this book will be the first of many linking literature to the writing traits.

To Janice, my great friend and colleague, who says, "Have you thought about saying it this way?" Or, "I have a copy of that." Thank you for always having the answers when I get stuck. How you do this, I don't know, but I'm so grateful every day to have you on the other end of the phone or e-mail.

Thank you to Terry Cooper, Judy deTuncq, Susan Kolwicz, and Joanna Davis-Swing of Scholastic who say, "Yes, it can be done." To Mary Sue Fordham who says, "Let me help." To Sam Culham who says, "I'm proud of you, Mom."

And finally, my deepest thanks to my friends Bridey Monterossi, Beth Sullivan, Ann Rader, and Janet Slocum who ask, "Aren't you finished with that book yet?" It's such a cliché, but you have been there for me every day. I don't know what to say other than thank you—it hardly seems adequate.

Cover design by Josué Castilleja
Interior design by Holly Grundon
Photographs: pages 4, 34, 58, and 105 by Michael C. York;
pages 12, 126, and 134 by James Levin/Studio Ten/SODA;
page 84 by Photodisc via SODA

ISBN 0-439-55687-2
Copyright © 2004 by The Writing Traits Company
All rights reserved. Published by Scholastic Inc.
Printed in China.

1 2 3 4 5 6 7 8 9 10   40   11 10 09 08 07 06 05 04